To Randy Courts and Jenny Laird — M. P. O. and W. O.

For Kier and Pia — G. P.

Authors' Note

Sleeping Bobby was inspired by the story of Sleeping Beauty first published in France in 1697 by Charles Perrault. Another version of "Sleeping Beauty," called "Little Briar-Rose," was retold in Germany in the early nineteenth century in *Household Stories* by the Brothers Grimm. Our story draws mainly upon the Grimms' tale.

Atheneum Books for Young Readers
An imprint of Simon & Schuster Children's
Publishing Division
1230 Avenue of the Americas
New York, New York 10020
Text copyright © 2005 by
Mary Pope Osborne and Will Osborne
Illustrations copyright © 2005 by Giselle Potter
All rights reserved, including the right of
reproduction in whole or in part in any form.
Book design by Lee Wade
The text for this book is set in OPTIPackardC.
The illustrations for this book are rendered
in pencil, ink, gouache, gesso, and watercolor.
Manufactured in China
First Edition
10 9 8 7 6 5 4 3 2 1

Library of Congress Cataloging-in-Publication Data
Osborne, Mary Pope.
Sleeping Bobby / Mary Pope Osborne and Will Osborne;
illustrated by Giselle Potter.— 1st ed.
p. cm.
"An Anne Schwartz Book."
Summary: A retelling of the Grimm tale featuring a
handsome prince who is put into a deep sleep by a curse
until he is awakened by the kiss of a brave princess.
ISBN 0-689-87668-8
(ISBN-13: 978-0-689-87668-4)
[1. Fairy tales. 2. Folklore—Germany.]
I. Osborne, Will. II. Potter, Giselle, ill.
III. Sleeping Beauty. English. IV. Title.
PZ8.O815Sl 2005
398.2—dc22
2004006346

Sleeping Bobby

Will Osborne and Mary Pope Osborne

Illustrated by Giselle Potter

AN ANNE SCHWARTZ BOOK

Atheneum Books for Young Readers

New York   London   Toronto   Sydney

Once upon a time a king and queen wanted a child very badly. Every day the queen would say to the king,

"Don't you wish we had a little one to share our kingdom with?"

And every day the king would answer,
"Yes, my dear, I do."

One day the king was swimming in the royal pond, when a frog hopped onto the bank.

"I am here to tell you that your wish will soon be granted," said the frog. "Within a year, you will have a baby boy."

"Why, thank you!" said the king, and he rushed home to tell the queen the good news.

A year later a baby boy was born to the royal couple. The child was so extraordinary and so delightful that the king and queen wanted him to have a very special name.

"How about Bob?"
asked the queen.

"Bob he shall be!"
replied the king.

To celebrate the birth of Bob, the
king and queen planned a huge feast. They
invited almost everyone in the realm, including
the kingdom's twelve Wise Women, for whom they set a
table all their own. In truth, there were thirteen Wise
Women in the kingdom, but since the queen had only
enough good china to serve twelve, one had to be left out.

On the night of the feast
each Wise Woman presented a gift to
Bob. One gave him kindness, another courage,
a third modesty. The gifts were all qualities
that anyone might wish for and admire.

Just as the twelfth Wise Woman
was about to bestow her gift, the
door of the royal nursery flew open,
and the thirteenth Wise Woman
burst into the room.

"How dare you have a feast and not invite *me!*" she shouted at the king and queen.

"There was a problem with the china," said the queen.

"Silence!"

said the thirteenth Wise Woman, who, in her rage, did not seem very wise at all. "Invited or not, I have a gift for Bob too. On his eighteenth birthday he shall prick his finger with a spindle and fall down dead!" And with that, she stormed out of the room, slamming the door behind her.

The king and queen and their guests were all horrified.

But then the twelfth Wise Woman, who had not yet presented her gift, stepped forward.

"Perhaps I can help," she said. "This shall be my gift to Bob.

On his eighteenth birthday he will not die, but fall into a deep sleep that will last for a hundred years."

The king and queen were silent for a moment. "Is that the best you can do?" the king finally asked.

"I am afraid it is," said the twelfth Wise Woman. "Alas, we are not allowed to completely undo each other's curses."

"I see," said the king. "Then I will have to take matters into my own hands."

The following day the king issued a proclamation. Spinning of any kind was strictly forbidden in the kingdom, and all spindles were to be destroyed at once.

"That should take care of it," he said to the queen.

"I certainly hope so," the queen replied.

With no spindles anywhere to be found and no spinning allowed, the thirteenth Wise Woman's curse was soon forgotten. Bob grew up to be kind, clever, modest, and *very* handsome. By the time he was a young man, he had so many good qualities that everyone who knew him admired him tremendously.

For Bob's eighteenth birthday, the king and queen planned a splendid birthday party. On the morning of the celebration they rode into town to buy the finest presents and provisions, leaving Bob on his own.

Among his other good qualities, Bob had great curiosity and a taste for adventure. There were many parts of the castle he had never explored. So, while his parents were out, he began wandering through deserted hallways and peeking into hidden rooms and parlors.

Eventually Bob came upon a mysterious staircase. "How peculiar!" he said. "I don't believe I've ever seen *this* before." He climbed the steep stairs to a small wooden door. A whirring sound came from the other side.

Bob pushed open the door.
Inside, an old woman sat spinning
flax at a large wooden wheel.

"Hello!" said Bob. "What on
earth is that?"

"It's a spinning wheel," said
the old woman. "Would you like
to try it?"

"Yes, please," said Bob, always polite and ready for adventure.
Bob sat down beside her. As soon as he touched the wheel's
spindle, a splinter pricked his finger.

Immediately Bob sank into
a deep, enchanted sleep.

So deep was his sleep that the entire castle fell under its spell. The king and queen, returning home from their party errands, collapsed in the front hall. The horse in the stable munching his oats, the sweeper in the courtyard sweeping the leaves, the dog in the doorway scratching his fleas,

the cook in the kitchen scolding the scullery maid, the flies in the pantry buzzing around the bread—all fell fast asleep where they munched, swept, scratched, scolded, or buzzed. The flames in all the hearths slept also. Even the wind slept, and the leaves of the trees.

As the castle slept and slept, a great hedge of thorns grew up around it. Years passed, and the thorn hedge grew higher and higher, until its brambles covered the entire castle, even the tallest towers.

Meanwhile rumors spread that a kind, clever, modest, and *very* handsome prince lay sleeping somewhere in a castle hidden by a giant thorny hedge. No one knew exactly where the castle was, or why a handsome prince was sleeping there. They only knew that the prince's name was Bob.

As rumors of Bob spread throughout the land, young women from far and wide began to search for him. A few found their way to the enchanted castle. But when they tried to pass through the hedge, they were stopped by the sharp, prickly thorns.

Nearly a hundred years passed. Then one day a kind, clever, modest, and *very* lovely princess set out into the world to seek her fortune. In her travels she often heard people speak of a very handsome prince named Bob who had been sleeping for ninety-nine years in a thorn-covered castle. She also heard that many young women had searched for Bob, but all had been stopped by the thorny hedge.

"If this Bob is all they say, it will take more than some shrubbery to keep *me* from meeting him," said the princess.

(Like Bob, the princess had great curiosity and a taste for adventure.)

Up and down the land, through woods and valleys, over fields and plains, the princess searched for the hidden castle. Finally she came upon the gigantic hedge she'd heard so much about.

As luck would have it, the princess arrived exactly one hundred years to the hour since Bob had pricked his finger. Before her very eyes, the thorns of the giant hedge turned to flowers and the branches beckoned her inside. When the princess got off her horse, the hedge parted to let her enter the castle grounds.

The princess soon realized that time had stopped for the mysterious castle.

She walked past the horse in the stable, the
sweeper in the courtyard, and the dog in the doorway. She
passed the cook in the kitchen, the flies on the bread,
and the king and queen in the front hall. All looked
exactly as they had a hundred years before when they
had fallen under the thirteenth Wise Woman's curse.

The princess wandered the still palace, winding through mysterious hallways, peeking into hidden rooms and parlors. At last she came to the staircase that led to the room in the tower where Bob slept.

She climbed the stairs and pushed open the door. . . .

There was Bob, lying on the bed, exactly where he had lain for a hundred years. "Oh, my," she breathed, "he is handsome!"

In fact, Bob was so handsome that the princess could not help herself—she leaned over and kissed him on the lips.

Bob opened his eyes and stared sleepily at the princess. "What time is it?" he said.

Bob and the princess fell deeply and immediately in love.

Holding hands, they
went downstairs and found
that all the castle had
awakened with Bob.

The horse was munching his oats, the sweeper was sweeping the leaves, the
dog was scratching his fleas, the cook was scolding the scullery maid, and the flies
were buzzing around the bread. The flames leapt in the hearth and the wind
whistled in the trees. The king and queen yawned and stretched.

The princess and Bob asked the king and queen if they could be married as soon as possible. And they were, that very afternoon.

Bob's birthday party became a wedding celebration, and the king and the queen and the princess and Bob and even the dog in the doorway lived happily ever after.